Baby Tiger Wants to Explore

Parent's Introduction

This book can be read with children in several different ways. You can read the book to them or, depending on their ability, they may be able to read the book to you. You can also take turns reading! Throughout the book, you will find words and phrases in big, bold text. If your child is just beginning to read, you might want to invite your child to participate in reading this text.

Your child may enjoy several readings of this story. With each reading, your child might see or focus on something new. As you read together, consider taking time to discuss the story and the information about the animals. Also, at the end of the story, we have included some fun questions to talk about together.

Baby Tiger Wants to Explore
A Photo Adventure™ Book

Author	Alice Greene
Editor	Elizabeth Bennett
Publishing Director	Chester Fisher
Creative Director	Simmi Sikka
Designer	Priya Chopra
Project Manager	Shekhar Kapur
Art Editor	Maria Janet

Picture Credits
t=top b=bottom r= right l=left
Front Cover: Mistock/iStockphoto-Andre Nantel/Shutterstock
Back Cover: David A. Northcott/Corbis; Half Title: Karen Givens/iStockphoto, Aldra/iStockphoto
3 Andre Nantel/Shutterstock; 4-5 Gerard Lacz/Photolibrary; 5b Purestock/Photolibrary; 6-7 Juniors Bildarchiv/Photolibrary;
7t Chanyut Sribuarawd/iStockphoto; 8-9 Image Source/Corbis; 9t Chanyut Sribuarawd/iStockphoto;
10b Mark Schroy/iStockphoto; 10-11: D. Robert & Lorri Franz/Corbis; 12-13 David A. Northcott/Corbis; 14-15 Dlillc/Corbis;
16b Sanjeev Gupta/Shutterstock; 16-17 Mike Hill/Photographer Choice/Getty Images; 18b Dawn Nichols/iStockphoto;
18-19 Corbis/Photolibrary; 20-21 Purestock/Photolibrary; 21t: Sharon Day/Shutterstock;
22-23 Jagdeep Rajput/Photographers Direct; 24: David A. Northcott/Corbis.

Published by Treasure Bay, Inc.
P.O. Box 119, Novato, CA 94948 USA

PRINTED IN SINGAPORE

Library of Congress Catalog Card Number: 2010921694

Hardcover ISBN-10: 1-60115-287-6
Hardcover ISBN-13: 978-1-60115-287-9
Paperback ISBN-10: 1-60115-288-4
Paperback ISBN-13: 978-1-60115-288-6

Visit us online at:
www.TreasureBayBooks.com

PR 07/10

It is calm and quiet in the **jungle.**

Suddenly, there's a rustle of leaves.

Who could it **be?**

It's a family of **tigers!**

Baby Tiger and his sister are playing with their mother.

FACT STOP

Tigers usually live in warm, thick forests. However, some tigers live in areas that are very cold and snowy.

5

A baby tiger is called a *cub.*

Wait!

Baby Tiger hears something!

Is there something moving
in the **grass?**

What could it be?

7

Could it be a **bug?**

Maybe it's a mouse!

Baby Tiger hurries
off to find out.

8

Jib ....

String with two studs ..

Create a crane
The crane's cab rotates on a 2x2 turntable piece. The cable is a string with studs that rests on a hinged jib.

2x2 turntable

Build it!

Record breakers

The **strongest crawler crane** lifts 300 tons (272 tonnes). That's about the same weight as 150 cars!

The **biggest bulldozer** had such a long blade, that four adult men could lie down end-to-end in it.

◀ Crawler crane
This handy vehicle lifts heavy loads. Crawler cranes roll slowly across building sites on tracks to transport their loads.

Tracks keep the crane steady on all types of terrain

.... **Driver's cab**

Drum roller

Engine is at the back of the vehicle ....

.. **Hook is raised and lowered on a strong cable**

Dump truck
Wide dump trucks carry rocks, sand, or earth around the building site. A big engine powers a hydraulic lift, which tilts the truck bed so that the load is emptied out.

Cab windows keep the dust out ...

Load is carried in the open bed

▲ Road roller
A road roller's massive, drum-shaped wheels are super-heavy. They can flatten earth or smooth out the surface of a newly laid road.

THIS TRUCK ROCKS!

· **Hinge**

On the racetrack

Speeding around a track, zipping through the air, or zooming down the ice, racing is fun. Each racing machine is different, but they are all built with one thing in mind—speed!

Record breakers

In 2010, Michael Pfister set the **world record** for luge speed at 96 mph (154 kph). That's faster than the average speed of a car.

The **world's first motor race** was held in France in 1894. It took the winning driver nearly seven hours to finish the 79-mile (127-km) course.

Build it!

Gray tap piece

Art of the kart
Combine small silver or gray parts at the back of the kart to make a complex-looking motor.

HEY, WAIT FOR ME!

Space for only one person

Body is close to the ground

Front bumper

▲ Go-kart

Small, swift go-karts race on twisted tracks. Most go-karts have soft tires that grip the track better than normal tires for more control.

WHAT AN "ICE" RIDE!

▶ Luge

This racing sled is called a "luge," which means "sled" in French. The rider lies flat on his or her back and pushes the luge forward to speed down an icy track.

Tight-fitting bodysuit

Luges have no brakes—racers use their feet to stop

Steel is the only part of the luge that touches the ice

Short fin helps the plane go faster

Carbon-fiber body makes the plane light and fast

◀ Racing plane

Air racing is not just about speed. Planes perform tricky turning maneuvers, too. The planes are super-light, and their smooth, sleek shape is designed to cut through the air easily.

Landing wheels are covered so air flows smoothly around them

Spoiler streamlines the shape so car goes faster

Secrets of spin
The plane's propeller slots onto a bar, with a 1x1 ring to hold it in place. Don't secure the propeller too tightly if you want it to spin around.

2x2x2 cone

Propeller piece

Bar piece

1x1 round plate with hole

Build it!

Stripes help viewers identify the car at high speeds

▲ Race car

Whether it's blazing around a track or a long-distance rally, car racing has been popular since the first motor vehicle was invented. Race cars are made for maximum speed and are driven by highly skilled drivers.

Smooth tire

Back in time

Charioteers competed standing up

Sometimes multiple horses pulled a chariot

Carriage was open at the back

Ancient Roman chariot races were fast and furious! Driven by one man and **pulled by horses**, chariots raced around oval-shaped racetracks.

Racing chariots had two wheels and were made of wood or wicker. They were light and maneuverable to get around tight bends.

15

Around the city

Cities are filled with vehicles traveling from place to place carrying passengers or goods. There are so many ways to get around busy city streets. With ice cream truck music and vehicle horns, there is plenty of noise, too!

Record breakers

Melbourne, Australia has the world's **biggest city tram network**, with around 500 trams and more than 1,700 stops.

In Brazil, the **world's longest bus** has three sections connected by pivoting joints. It's about the same length as six family cars.

Ice cream machine

Loudspeaker plays music

Serving hatch

THIS IS THE COOLEST TRUCK IN TOWN!

Ice cream truck ▲

The ice cream truck plays a cheerful chiming song to let everyone know that sweet treats are on the way. Built-in freezers keep frozen treats cool, even on a hot summer day.

Handlebars for steering

◀ Tricycle

Riding through the city park on a tricycle is fun. With three wheels, it's easier to stay balanced on a tricycle than on a two-wheeled bike.

Two back wheels help balance the tricycle

... Single front wheel

Roof can be folded down

Room for two passengers .....

Auto rickshaw ▶

These small passenger carriers are great for zipping through busy and narrow urban streets. They are designed for short journeys.

Open sides

Overhead electric cable

Pivoting joint for going around bends

Rod, called a pantograph, picks up electricity from the cable

▲ Tram

Trams glide along rails in the road. They run on electric power from overhead cables. Trams are good city vehicles because they help stop the roads from getting too busy with cars.

Passenger door

Build it!

A clear view
All the windows of the bus are made from windshield pieces that support the roof above. Other clear pieces are used for the doors.

2x4x2 windshield

Two sets of doors for faster boarding and disembarking

Light flashes when the bus turns right

▲ City bus

Buses roll along, stopping at bus stops to let people on and off. Some streets have special bus lanes, so buses can move around the city easily even at the busiest times.

Light is on when taxi is free

Passengers sit in the rear

Traffic light tells vehicles when it's safe to go

◄ Taxi

A taxi is driven by a professional driver who takes passengers to where they need to go. The passenger pays a fare based on the distance and time the journey takes.

17

Rolling through time

When humans put wheels on the first cart, they could never have guessed what would happen next! For thousands of years, the invention of the wheel has made all kinds of vehicles possible—from a simple bicycle to a car that drives itself.

An axle fits through the hole to join the wheel to a cart

3500 BCE
Wheels
Before they helped vehicles roll along, wheels were used to help potters make pots. Three hundred years after these were invented, lighter wheels were attached to chariots.

Early wheels were solid disks of wood

1860s
Steam tractors
Steam-powered tractors replaced horses for heavy farm work. They were useful but were eventually replaced by smaller, more affordable gas-powered tractors.

Driver's seat

Flywheel powered a machine to separate grain from wheat ...

1920s
Family cars
The first gas-powered car was made in 1886, and it changed the way people traveled. By the 1920s, factories worldwide produced millions of affordable, reliable cars for families to use.

Early cars often had open tops

Wheels were made of wood ......

.... Each driver chooses a colorful theme

1980s
Monster trucks
Early monster trucks were modified pickup trucks with huge wheels. They appeared in special races and shows.

Giant tires for stunts ...

2010s
Self-driving cars
Computers started driving cars in the 21st century. Cameras and sensors on a car send data to a computer, enabling the vehicle to steer around obstacles and operate safely.

Sensor scans the area to keep the vehicle safe ......

Camera

18

Full steam sideways!

The steam car is built around a sideways angle plate, with 1x1 round plates for wheels built onto bricks with side studs.

Bar secures lid on barrel

1x1 headlight brick

1x2/2x2 angled plate

1x1 brick with two side studs

I'M READY TO ROLL!

1760s

Steam-powered cars

The earliest road cars were steam-powered carriages. They were slow, and their heavy steam boilers had to be refilled with coal every 15 minutes.

Boiler

Throttle lever controlled speed

Tiller for steering

1810s

Bicycles

The first-ever bicycle was known as the "dandy horse." It had no pedals. To move the wheels, the rider sat on the saddle and walked or ran on the ground.

Saddle

Wooden frame

1950s

Flying cars

These amazing vehicles were plastic cars with detachable wings, a propeller, and a tail. They could convert from road to flight mode in just a few minutes.

Folding wings

Room for driver and one passenger

1970s

Hydraulic excavators

Until the 1970s, most diggers used wire cables to move the boom. The invention of hydraulics allowed fluid inside the machine to power the boom instead. This made excavators more powerful.

Bucket

Boom

Continuous track

Wings and wheels

The wheels of the flying car are 1x1 round tiles on LEGO® Technic half pins in plates with rings beneath.

LEGO Technic half pin

1x1 round tile

2x2 plate with rings beneath

Underneath the ground

Most vehicles travel above ground—on land, on water, or in the air. But some vehicles are specially made to move people or do important jobs under the Earth's surface.

THIS LOADER IS "MINE"!

Scoop

Flat body for low ceilings

Mine loader ▲
Specialized trucks help mine-workers move coal and rocks deep underground. Designed to operate in cramped spaces, the trucks are low and easy to drive through narrow spaces.

Tough tires are hard to puncture

Passenger carriage

Large windows

Record breakers

Beijing, China is home to the **world's busiest subway system**. It carries almost 10 million passengers every day.

The **biggest roadheader** in the world weighs a ground-crushing 135 tons (122 tonnes)—the same as 20 African elephants!

▲ Subway train
In some big cities, the quickest transportation network is hidden under the street. Subway trains travel through a network of tunnels, bypassing the traffic and crowds on the streets above.

Train operator's cab

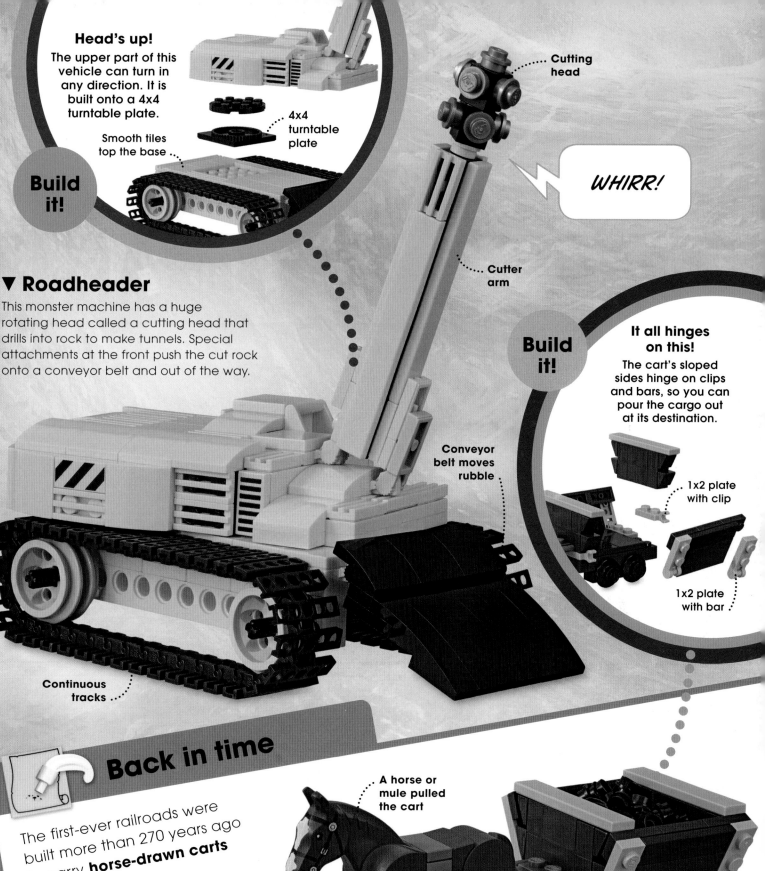

Head's up!
The upper part of this vehicle can turn in any direction. It is built onto a 4x4 turntable plate.

Smooth tiles top the base

4x4 turntable plate

Build it!

Cutting head

WHIRR!

Cutter arm

▼ Roadheader
This monster machine has a huge rotating head called a cutting head that drills into rock to make tunnels. Special attachments at the front push the cut rock onto a conveyor belt and out of the way.

Conveyor belt moves rubble

Build it!

It all hinges on this!
The cart's sloped sides hinge on clips and bars, so you can pour the cargo out at its destination.

1x2 plate with clip

1x2 plate with bar

Continuous tracks

Back in time

The first-ever railroads were built more than 270 years ago to carry **horse-drawn carts** through mines.

The **carts' wheels had grooves** that sat on wooden or iron rails. This made the heavy carts easy to pull along the tracks.

A horse or mule pulled the cart

Carts were made of wood

Down at the docks

At the docks, boats and ships carry goods in and out of the harbor. Land vehicles then help move the goods from sea-going vessels to stores and warehouses.

Towboat has a flat front to push the barge

Shipping container

Wide, flat shape helps it to float even when filled with heavy cargo

▲ Barge

Barges have flat bottoms and wide decks to carry heavy loads of goods along rivers and canals. Most barges are pushed by towboats or pulled by tugboats.

Build it!

A tow in the water

The tug's towline is a drum piece on a LEGO® Technic axle. Bricks with holes hold it in place but still allow it to turn.

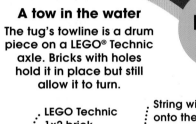

- **LEGO Technic 1x2 brick with hole**
- **String winds onto the drum**
- **LEGO Technic axle**
- **Drum**

Mainmast

Steel towing rope

Reel

Hull made of steel

Tugboat ◄

In a crowded port, it's not easy for big ships to maneuver, but powerful tugboats can. Using a strong towline, tugboats pull larger ships to where they need to be.

HOOONK!

22

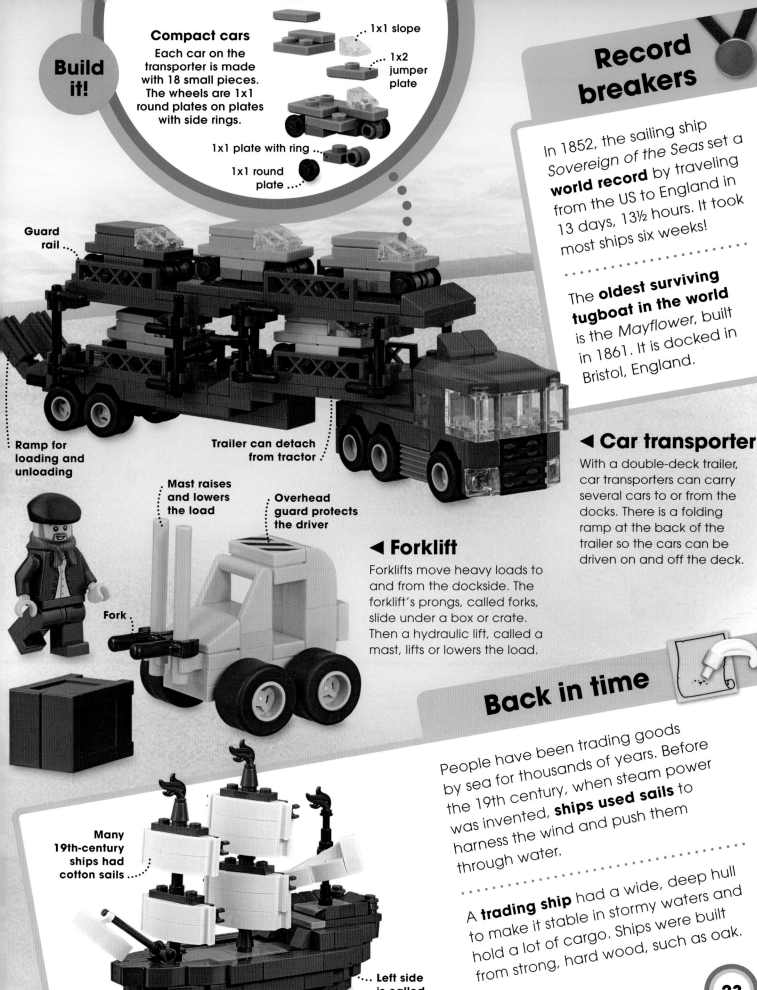

Build it!

Compact cars

Each car on the transporter is made with 18 small pieces. The wheels are 1x1 round plates on plates with side rings.

1x1 slope

1x2 jumper plate

1x1 plate with ring

1x1 round plate

Guard rail

Ramp for loading and unloading

Trailer can detach from tractor

Mast raises and lowers the load

Overhead guard protects the driver

Fork

◀ Forklift

Forklifts move heavy loads to and from the dockside. The forklift's prongs, called forks, slide under a box or crate. Then a hydraulic lift, called a mast, lifts or lowers the load.

Many 19th-century ships had cotton sails

Left side is called port side

Record breakers

In 1852, the sailing ship *Sovereign of the Seas* set a **world record** by traveling from the US to England in 13 days, 13½ hours. It took most ships six weeks!

The **oldest surviving tugboat in the world** is the *Mayflower*, built in 1861. It is docked in Bristol, England.

◀ Car transporter

With a double-deck trailer, car transporters can carry several cars to or from the docks. There is a folding ramp at the back of the trailer so the cars can be driven on and off the deck.

Back in time

People have been trading goods by sea for thousands of years. Before the 19th century, when steam power was invented, **ships used sails** to harness the wind and push them through water.

A **trading ship** had a wide, deep hull to make it stable in stormy waters and hold a lot of cargo. Ships were built from strong, hard wood, such as oak.

23

In the water

Most of the planet is covered with ocean, so there are plenty of vehicles made to travel through water. Watercraft carry people and goods all over the world.

Pilot house

Struts to keep the craft stable

Front foils

Rear foils

▲ Hydrofoil

A hydrofoil skims above the water on foils. As the boat speeds up, the foils lift it clear of the waves. With less drag from the water, the craft can move at fast speeds.

Make it shipshape
Build the sides of the ship's hull separately, then attach them using bricks with side studs.

Build it!

Five 1x2 bricks with two side studs

1x2 curved slope

Porthole

Lifebo

Swimming pool

Cruise ship ▲

These floating hotels take tourists on fancy trips to vacation destinations. Some ships are so big, they are like mini-cities—with restaurants, movie theaters, and stores.

Thruster propels the craft forward

Thick-walled window

◀ Submersible

Scientists use submersibles to explore and map the underwater world. These tough craft are specially designed to withstand the pressing weight of deep water.

Robotic arm

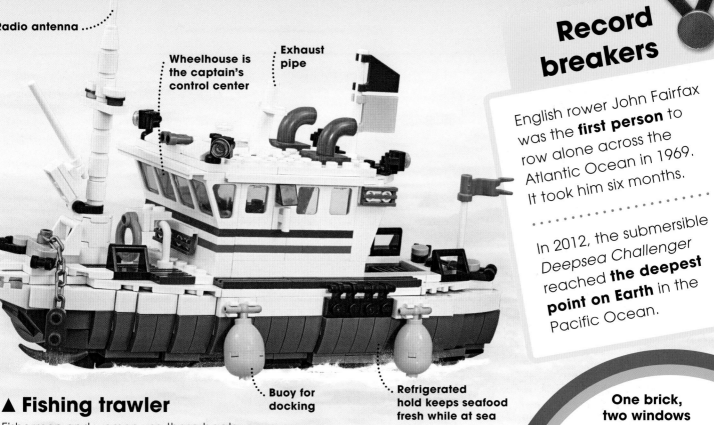

Radio antenna ·····

Wheelhouse is the captain's control center

Exhaust pipe

Record breakers

English rower John Fairfax was the **first person** to row alone across the Atlantic Ocean in 1969. It took him six months.

In 2012, the submersible *Deepsea Challenger* reached **the deepest point on Earth** in the Pacific Ocean.

Buoy for docking

Refrigerated hold keeps seafood fresh while at sea

▲ Fishing trawler

Fishermen and women use these boats to fish all over the world. The boats help catch and carry seafood, such as fish and crab, and take it back to shore.

ROW, ROW, ROW YOUR BOAT . . .

One brick, two windows

Use headlight bricks as micro-scale portholes, or turn them around to make square windows.

1x1 headlight brick

1x1 headlight brick

Rowboat ▶

A rower uses a pair of oars to power a rowboat. As the rower pulls the oars through the water, the force pushes the boat forward.

Build it!

Oar is flat at one end

Rowlock keeps the oar in place

Back in time

In the 19th century, the **steamboat** was the fastest boat on the water.

It was powered by a steam engine that **drove a large wheel**. As it turned, the wheel's paddles pushed through the water, moving the boat forward.

Funnel ·····

Paddle wheel

Paddle blade

Sailing through time

Traveling on or under the water has been an important way to get around for thousands of years. From ancient log canoes to vast, floating vacation villages, cruise through the long history of water vehicles.

Around 8000 BCE
Dugout canoes
Thousands of years ago, humans made simple canoes from logs. Stone Age fishermen cut down and hollowed out the tree trunks with sharpened flint rocks.

Canoes were made from wood, such as linden ...

... Room for up to eight people

800s CE
Viking longships
The Vikings built ships to take them long distances from their home in Scandinavia. These boats could operate equally well on the high seas or in shallow rivers.

Shield to protect oarsmen

Hull carved from one large oak tree

Lookout post is called the crow's nest ...

Different-shaped sails make the ship fast and easy to steer

1500s
Sailing ships
Explorers from Europe used fast sailing ships called caravels to explore new lands. With lots of sails, the boats were powered only by wind and the sea currents.

1950s
Hovercraft
The hovercraft skims across the water's surface on a big cushion filled with air. It can also travel over other surfaces, including ice and sand.

Navigation and communications antennae

Inflatable cushion called a skirt

2010s
Colossal cruisers
Modern cruise ships can carry thousands of vacationers at a time. These huge ships have onboard parks, restaurants, and even ice-skating rinks!

Back of a ship is the stern

Multistory decks ...

Build it!

Plain sailing
This sailboat is built sideways. Only the mast stands upright, built onto a 1x1 round plate with bar and hole.

1x1 round plate with bar and hole

I'M DIVING INTO HISTORY!

Travelers steered and moved the rafts with a wooden oar

Reed held the logs together

Broad cloth sail

3100s BCE
Egyptian sailboats
The Ancient Egyptians were the first people to use sails on their vessels. The sails caught the wind, allowing boats to travel faster along the slow-flowing River Nile.

Lookout position

Around 5000 BCE
Log rafts
The first rafts were built in Southeast Asia. They were made from logs and tied together with reeds. Explorers used these craft to travel as far as Australia!

Rudder for steering

Oar

1620s
Early submersibles
The first-ever underwater craft was built in England and launched in the River Thames. It was powered by 12 oarsmen and made from wood and oiled leather.

1840s
Steam-powered ships
Steam-powered iron ships transformed the world of shipping. These powerful vessels could travel quickly, making journeys in about half the time of a sailing ship.

Foldable mast

Funnel

Build it!

The right shape
The main sub build is only one stud wide, but 1x3 plates on both sides give it a rounder shape.

1x3 plate

Joystick

Down on the farm

Many farmers rely on specialized machines to help them grow plants and raise animals. Modern farm vehicles combine power and technology to perform jobs with maximum speed and efficiency.

Record breakers

The Big Bud 747 is claimed to be the **world's biggest tractor**. It has eight enormous tires and weighs 30 times more than a family car.

American blacksmith John Deere invented the first-ever steel plow in 1837. It could **handle even the toughest soil**, making life much easier for farmers.

Combine harvester ▼

This mighty machine combines lots of harvesting jobs in one. It cuts crops, then separates them into grain and straw. The straw is ejected at the back, ready to be made into hay bales.

Grain storage tank

Grain unloading pipe

Front attachment is called the header

Cutter bar cuts the crop

Surrounding windows for maximum visibility

Hood protects the engine

Build it!

Pin it!
The back wheels of the tractor connect to LEGO® Technic connector pegs. The front wheels click onto smaller wheel connectors.

LEGO Technic connector peg

2x2 plate with wheel connectors

▲ Tractor

Every farm needs a tractor. This heavyweight helper can do all kinds of tasks, from lifting loads to plowing fields or pulling trailers.

Huge, chunky wheels don't slip in the mud

Seed-planting plane ▶

Planting large areas with crops, such as wheat, beans, rye, and corn, is fast work with a plane. Seed-planting planes drop seeds over a wide area. This process is called aerial seeding.

"HAY"—IT'S A PLANE!

Small cockpit for pilot

Seeds stored in a hold

Seeds released below the fuselage

Propeller

Hay bales

Insulated tank keeps the milk cool

Access hatch for checking the load

Hose attaches to rear to fill tank

Build it!

Drum kit

The tanker drum connects to a brick with a hole and rests in a channel made from a dozen 1x1 slopes.

2x2 dome

1x2 brick with hole

Two rows of 1x1 slopes

▲ Milk tanker

A milk tanker carries milk from a dairy farm to a factory. Its steel container holds up to 6,600 gallons (30,000 liters) of milk—enough to fill about 200 bathtubs.

Back in time

Before tractors, **horses pulled heavy plows** across fields to turn the soil and get it ready for planting.

The farmer held stilts to **steer the plow** and control the depth of the furrows, which were rows of cuts in the soil.

Harness connects to plow

Stilts

Moldboard pushes the soil to one side

Plowshare cuts into the soil

29

Built for fun

Many vehicles are useful with special jobs to do, but some are made just for people to have a great time. Fast or slow, there are tons of fun vehicles out there to enjoy!

> A SIDECAR HAS ONLY ONE WHEEL!

LEGO Technic axle pin

2x2 plate with holes

LEGO Technic axle pin

Spare tire

Fender

Sidecar link

Connection
This motorcycle has an axle connector on the side, so you can add on a sidecar using LEGO® Technic pieces.

Build it!

> THIS IS "WHEELY" GREAT!

▲ Sidecar
A passenger sidecar attaches to the main frame of a scooter or motorcycle. There is one passenger seat and often a little compartment to store small items, such as food.

Back in time

Cycling was popular in the 1870s. The penny-farthing, or high-wheeler, had a **huge front wheel**. The big wheel allowed the bike to travel faster than a standard bicycle.

The bike was high-tech for its time. The frame was made from hollow metal tubes, making it much **lighter and easier** to steer than the solid iron bikes before it.

Passenger sat high off the ground

Trailing wheel

Rubber tire instead of wood

I'M HAVING A BALL!

Space for golf clubs

... Steering wheel

Batteries are under the seat

▲ Golf cart

Golf carts carry golfers and their equipment from hole to hole. The carts are built low to the ground to help them stay upright on bumpy terrain. Most are powered by rechargeable batteries.

Personal watercraft ▶

A thruster at the back of this vehicle sucks in water, then squirts it out with force. This pushes the watercraft forward.

Record breakers

In 2005 in Florida, 3,321 golf carts took part in the **longest-ever golf cart parade**. It took nearly four hours for all the carts to roll past the counting point.

In 2002, Alvaro de Marichalar became the first person to **ride a personal watercraft** across the Atlantic Ocean. He rode 12 hours every day for four months.

Steering yoke

Jet thruster

Cooler

Bumper

THERE'S NO ENGINE ON A KAYAK–JUST ME AND MY PADDLE!

◄ Kayak

Kayaking is a fun way to glide through water. The kayaker uses a paddle with a blade at each end to steer the narrow boat.

Kayaker's seat is called the cockpit

Most kayaks are made of plastic

Bowline for docking

Bow and narrow
The kayak's bowline is a string with studs. It loops around the tiles that make the slender sides.

... String with two studs

1x6 tile

1x1 brick with side stud

Build it!

Up in the air

People have devised many different ways of getting vehicles to fly. The first-ever airplane flight lasted only three seconds. Today, some aircraft can fly for thousands of miles without stopping to refuel.

NEEOW!

Record breakers

The **largest blimp** ever built was *Graf Zeppelin II*. The blimp, built in the 1930s, was three times longer than a jumbo jet.

The **tiniest unmanned aerial vehicle** is smaller than a quarter. It was designed to carry out search-and-rescue missions.

Spreader bar ·······

······· Propeller

Float ·····

▲ Seaplane

Instead of wheels, the seaplane has two floats so it can take off from and land on water. They are mostly used in areas with few airfields.

Lightweight frame ·······

Spinning blades keep the drone in the air

······· Remote control

Drone ▲

An unmanned aerial vehicle (UAV), or drone, is a flying machine that's operated by remote control. Drones carry special equipment to film the land below or monitor weather. Some even deliver packages!

Build it!

······· Jumper plate to center wings

······· Transparent small radar dish piece

In a spin

A clear dish piece on the front of the seaplane creates the illusion of a propeller spinning so fast it is almost invisible.

Ducted fan
for steering

Helium-filled
balloon

Rear propeller
moves the ship
through the air

▲ Blimp

The blimp is filled with a gas
called helium that's lighter
than air, making the ship float.
Propellers move it forward
and keep it on course.

Passenger
cabin

Build it!

Horse power

The wings and tail of
this old-fashioned plane
are connected by two
LEGO® pieces more often
used to make horse carts.

Horse cart
harness

Telescope
pieces

Flame-resistant
material

Hot air balloon ▶

A gas burner under the
balloon heats the air inside it.
As the air gets hotter, the
balloon rises. To travel back
down, the pilot pulls a cord to
let air out of the balloon.

Basket for the pilot
and passengers

Bottom of envelope
is called the skirt

Back in time

More than 100 years ago, the first
powered planes took to the skies.
The double sets of wings provided lifting
power and made the plane easy to steer.

To fly the plane, the pilot **lay flat on
his stomach** on top of the lower wing.
He moved a small set of wings at the
front to make the plane go up or down.

Wings were
made of wood
and cloth

Rear

Front

Thin struts
connected the wings

At the airport

There are many vehicles at an airport besides airplanes. Each airport vehicle has a special task to do and is designed to make sure that every plane is ready to take off or land.

Record breakers

Jumbo jets have a wingspan of 250 ft (76.2 m). That means **eight double-decker buses** could line up from wing to wing!

The **world's largest fuel tanker** is made for airports. It holds 15,000 gallons (68,000 liters) of fuel—almost twice as much as normal road fuel tankers.

THESE CARS CAN CARRY HUNDREDS OF BAGS AT ONCE.

Pose your hose
The fuel truck's rigid hose is made from two L-shaped bars. They are connected by a tube holder with clip.

L-shaped bar

Tube holder with clip

1x2 plate with top clip

2x2 turntable

Build it!

Hose delivers fuel to the plane

Fuel gauge

Filter

▲ Aircraft refueler

Airplanes need fuel before they can take off. The fuel truck has a hose to connect it to an underground jet fuel store. The truck delivers the fuel to a plane's tanks.

Covers protect baggage in bad weather

Car

Tug

▲ Baggage car

Luggage is loaded onto baggage cars. The cars are linked together and pulled to the plane by a tug vehicle. Each car has an automatic parking brake for extra safety.

Top deck

▲ Jumbo jet

This flying giant is designed for long-distance passenger flights. Double-decker "superjumbo" jets like this one have room for more than 850 people in their cabins.

Elevator

Four engines power the plane

Transfer shuttle ▼

Planes often have to park a long way from the passenger terminal. The shuttle bus transfers passengers safely to and from the aircraft. Inside, there is space for passengers and their carry-on luggage.

Driver-controlled safety doors

Passenger seating

Rear panel

Refrigerated food crate

Ramp to the plane door

◄ Catering truck

Airline meals are prepared on the ground and delivered to the aircraft. The truck's body can be raised up to the door of the plane so that the crew can unload the food easily.

Hydraulic lift raises and lowers the container

Up and down

The ramp to the plane door can be raised and lowered using two 1x2 hinge bricks.

1x2 grille

1x4 white brick

1x2 hinge brick

Build it!

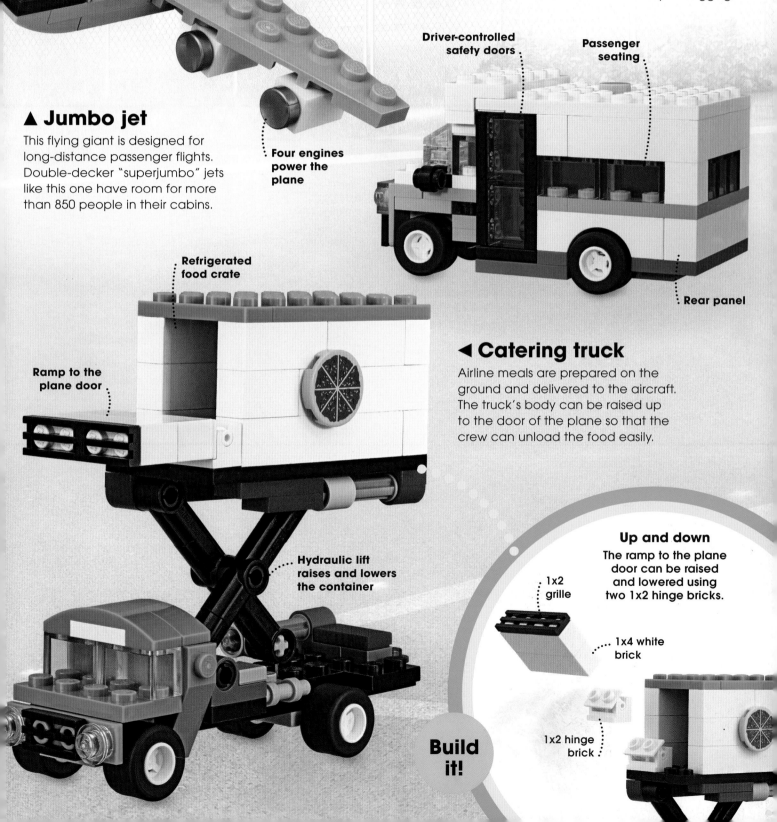

Flying through time

For hundreds of years, people looked up at the birds and wished they could fly, too. Eventually, inventors found clever ways to get airborne. Today, flying is part of everyday life for millions of people.

Balloon, called an envelope, made of silk

Passenger area

1780s
Hot air balloons
The first hot air balloons were developed in France. They allowed people to take to the sky for the first time ever.

Stabilizer helped control the plane

1910s
Monoplanes
In the 1920s, engineers developed single-wing planes called monoplanes. The machines were faster and sturdier than earlier double-winged planes and could travel longer distances.

Wheels for take-off and landing

Tail rotor steered helicopter

Rotor

1930s
Helicopters
Ideas for an aircraft that could lift straight into the air were first drawn up about 500 years ago. In the 1930s, the first helicopters took to the air with spinning blades called a rotor. Rotors let helicopters take off and land vertically.

Some designs had no closing doors

2010s
Drones
Flying drones, also called unmanned aerial vehicles, are piloted from the ground. This means the machines can travel to places that manned vehicles cannot, such as close to active volcanoes.

Camera can film the ground below

Lightweight frame

2x2 round plate with hooks

Small radar dish

Build it!

Make a drone of your own
Not all drones have four propellers. So even if you don't have a plate with four hooks, you can still build a realistic drone.

Bird-shaped cloth wing

Clip your wings
It takes just 10 pieces to make this biplane, including two kinds of plates with side clips.

···· **1x1 plate with clip**

···· **1x2 plate with clip**

Build it!

1850s
Gliders
Early glider engineers studied birds to learn how they stayed in the air. The machines they developed had angled wings, called airfoils, which caught more air than flat wings.

Wooden frame

1900s
Engine-powered airplanes
The earliest engine-powered planes had basic engines and could travel short distances easily. Their designs were inspired by successful gliders.

Rear rudder turned the plane

Elevators made the plane go up or down

1950s
Passenger jets
The development of the jet engine meant that airplanes could fly faster and farther than ever before. Air travel became a common way for lots of people to travel long distances.

Main body called a fuselage

2010s
Personal flyers
Most personal flyers, or jet packs, available today are powered by gas engines. These compact vehicles are designed to transport a solo pilot over a short distance.

Thrusters provide power to get airborne

Hand control

Jet engine sits under the wing

TAKE-OFF WAS EASY—NOW HOW DO I LAND THIS THING?

In the snow

Snow vehicles are tough and made to move through the worst wintry conditions. They can travel through snow, ice, strong winds, numbing cold, and swirling blizzards.

GETTING AROUND IN THIS WEATHER IS "SNOW" JOKE!

Record breakers

The Iditarod is the **longest dog-sled race** in the world. Teams of 16 huskies and a driver race 1,049 miles (1,688 km) over the frozen ground of Alaska.

In 1977, the Russian icebreaker *Arktika* became the **first surface ship** to reach the North Pole.

Handlebars for steering

Ski runner

Continuou track grip the ice an snow

Snowmobile ▲

The snowmobile has a powerful engine, continuous tracks, and ski runners that curve upward. The runners stop the vehicle from plowing into the snow.

Very high-frequency antenna

Crane at front and rear for lifting gear onto the ship

Pointed bow crushes ice

▲ Icebreaker ship

When it's so cold that even the sea freezes, the icebreaker clears a path for other ships. Its shape and extra-strong construction means it can power through ice that's 9 ft (2.8 m) deep—that's a bit deeper than an Olympic-size swimming pool!

Double hull gives the boat two watertight layers

Arctic articulation

A notched string with end studs links the sled to the dogs. Each dog wears a small bracket piece connected to a sideways 1x1 plate with a top clip.

Minifigure neck bracket

Notched string with end studs

Build it!

TO GET A DOG SLED TEAM TO GO, SAY "MUSH!"

Sled bag carries cargo

The driver stands on foot boards

Tugline

Husky sled ▲

In the Arctic, teams of hardworking husky dogs pull heavy loads in sleds. The sleds have skilike runners designed to glide easily over ice and snow.

Powerful light for plowing in limited visibility

▶ Snow plow

Even after a heavy snowstorm, the massive might of the snow plow soon clears the way. Its huge blade pushes snow and ice off the road.

Snow tires so the plow doesn't get stuck

Curved blade pushes snow to the side

Back in time

Driver and passenger seating

Curved shield

Reins

Horse-drawn sleighs were built for speed, with lightweight bodies and slim runners for gliding over packed snow. Sleighs were used to carry passengers and deliver the mail.

Passengers sat behind a **curved shield** to protect them from spray kicked up by the horses.

Runner glides over snow

Over rough terrain

When the going gets tough, these machines really get going! Some vehicles are designed or modified to handle all kinds of challenging off-road terrain, from sands to swamplands.

Roof protects passengers from the hot sun

Grille allows air to enter so engine doesn't overheat

All-terrain tire

SEE YA LATER, ALLIGATOR!

Steering
The skimmer's two propellers slot onto a nozzle piece. A claw fits onto the nozzle handle to make a steering lever.

Nozzle

Claw piece

Propeller

Propeller

1x2 jumper plate

Build it!

▲ Safari truck
An off-road safari truck has rugged tires and four-wheel drive to cope with desert dunes, flash floods, and rocky river beds. The body is long, flat, and open for wildlife-spotting.

Propeller

▼ Airboat
This boat is perfect for skimming through shallow water, such as swamps. Instead of an underwater engine, it is powered by a big fan, which pushes the boat forward.

Boat made of lightweight material, such as aluminum

Driver controls the boat from the back seat

Flat bottom for shallow water

40

Nozzle piece ..... •· Tube holder with clip

Unlocking the cage
Nozzle pieces and tube holders with clips combine to make the protective roll cage of this dune buggy.

Build it!

Record breakers

The world record for the **longest airboat journey** was set in the US, when two sailors completed a 1,100-mile (1,770-km) trip from Florida to New York City. The trip lasted 13 days.

The **fastest amphibious** vehicle in the world is the WaterCar Python. This water- and land-going car has a top speed of 60 mph (96 kph) on water.

•· Support frame made from steel tubes

Engine at the rear ...·

·.. Body made of fiberglass

▲ Dune buggy
Many vehicles struggle to drive over sand. Dune buggies have a simple design with a lightweight body and wide, soft tires to help them grip the sand.

Radio antenna

◄ Amphibious bus
On the road, this sightseeing vehicle is an ordinary tourist bus. However, the vehicle's watertight body lets it slip into the water for a river cruise, too!

Captain operates the vehicle from the cab ...·

Watertight hull

Tires can be deflated from the cab for driving over sand

Goods on the go

On land, over water, and in the air, vehicles transport goods from place to place. They carry big and small loads of everything imaginable, from electronics to food—and even this book!

Extra-large hold can carry vehicles or even other aircraft

Cargo door

Jet engine

Cargo plane ▲

Inside a cargo plane is a huge storage space called the hold. On some planes, the nose or tail opens so that goods can be loaded and stored in the hold.

Horn

Driver's cab

Box car

Pilot keeps tracks clear of debris

Diesel engine

Loading door

Hold for freight

▲ Freight train

Powerful diesel engines pull goods over long distances. Some trains use more than one engine. Freight trains can be made up of nine engines and more than 300 freight cars!

Hydraulic crane

Logging truck ◄

This truck carries large loads of cut-down trees. The truck transports the logs to a sawmill, where special machines cut them into planks.

Claw places logs on the truck's bed

Build it!

Tube with bar

T-bar

1x2 plate with clip

1x2 plate with two bars

Robot arm

Claw piece

Strong lifting arm

All kinds of different bars and clips combine to make the logging truck's crane arm.

Supports stop the logs from rolling off

1x3 plate

1x2 jumper plate

One container can hold 6,000 shoe boxes

Bridge is positioned high up to see over the stacks of containers

Build it!

Container ship ▶

Stacked high with massive metal boxes, container ships move freight over water. Each container is the same size and shape. This means they can be stacked like building blocks to make use of as much space as possible.

Containers fill the hull below deck

I HOPE THAT BOX CAR IS FULL OF COFFEE.

Fuel tanker

Trailer

Record breakers

The **world's largest container ship** can carry 21,413 containers. At 1,312 ft (400 m) long, five jumbo jets can line up on its deck.

The **largest cargo plane** is the Antonov An-225. It was designed to carry a space shuttle and has 32 wheels on its landing gear.

Tractor unit

Four rear wheels support the heavy trailer

▲ Semi-truck

A semi-truck hauls goods on the road. Freight is packed in the long trailer behind the tractor unit, which contains the engine and the driver's cab.

The truck bends at this joint so it can steer around corners

43

Wheels

Cart wheel

Train wheel

Large wheel without tire

1x1 round plate

Wheel connectors

LEGO Technic cross axle with groove

Controls

Console with wheel

Joystick

Tap

Windows

Windshield

Transparent 1x2x2 panel

Details

Binoculars

Curved tube

Small propeller

1x2 grille

2x4x1 brick with screen

1x2 grille slope

Lights

Transparent red lamp with bar

Build basics

Every build starts with a single piece—even the most complex-looking ones. Whether you want to build a car, a train, a ship, or a spacecraft, begin by thinking about its size and shape before picking the perfect first piece.

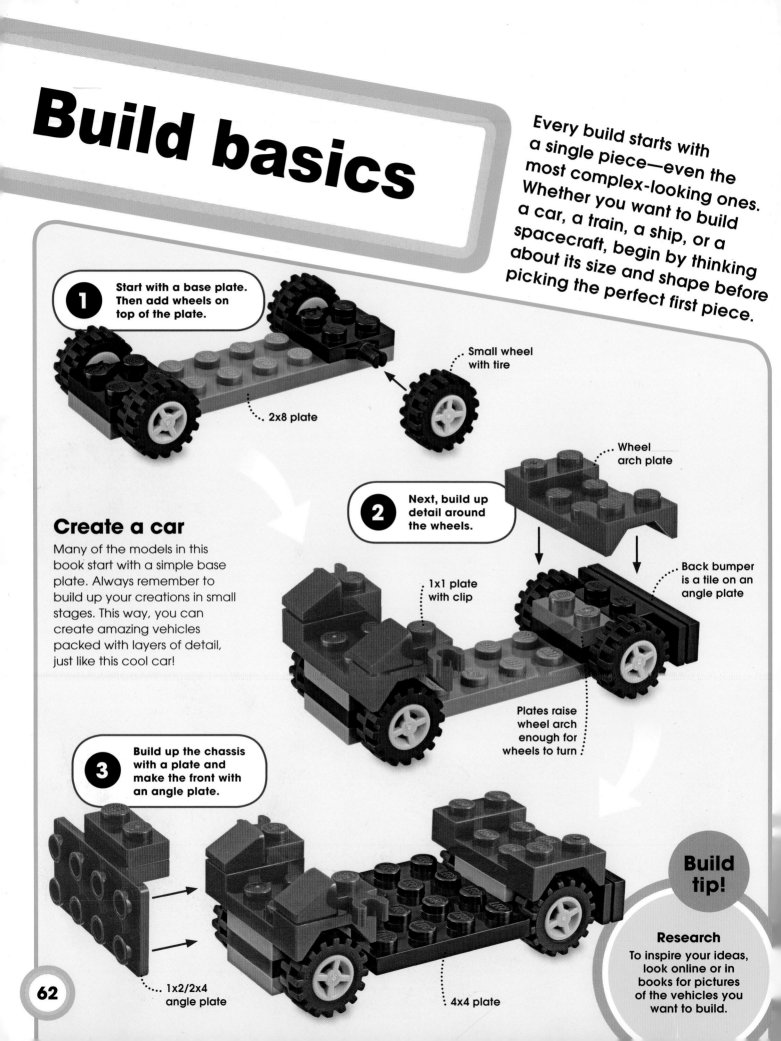

1 Start with a base plate. Then add wheels on top of the plate.

Small wheel with tire

2x8 plate

Create a car

Many of the models in this book start with a simple base plate. Always remember to build up your creations in small stages. This way, you can create amazing vehicles packed with layers of detail, just like this cool car!

Wheel arch plate

2 Next, build up detail around the wheels.

1x1 plate with clip

Back bumper is a tile on an angle plate

Plates raise wheel arch enough for wheels to turn

3 Build up the chassis with a plate and make the front with an angle plate.

1x2/2x4 angle plate

4x4 plate

Build tip!

Research
To inspire your ideas, look online or in books for pictures of the vehicles you want to build.

62

Build tip!

Organize your bricks

Save time by organizing your bricks into colors and types before you start building.

4 Use plates to build up the middle section.

Front lights and grille are built onto the angle plate

1x1 round plates make door handles

5 Level out the top of the build with plates.

1x6 plate

2x4 plate

2x2 curved slope

Build tip!

Be creative

If you don't have the perfect piece, find a creative solution! Look for a different piece that can create a similar effect.

Transparent 1x2 brick

Transparent 2x2 slope

6 Add windows and a roof.

Build tip!

Have fun

Don't worry if your model goes wrong. Turn it into something else or start again. The fun is in the building!

1x1 tiles as side-view mirrors provide more detail

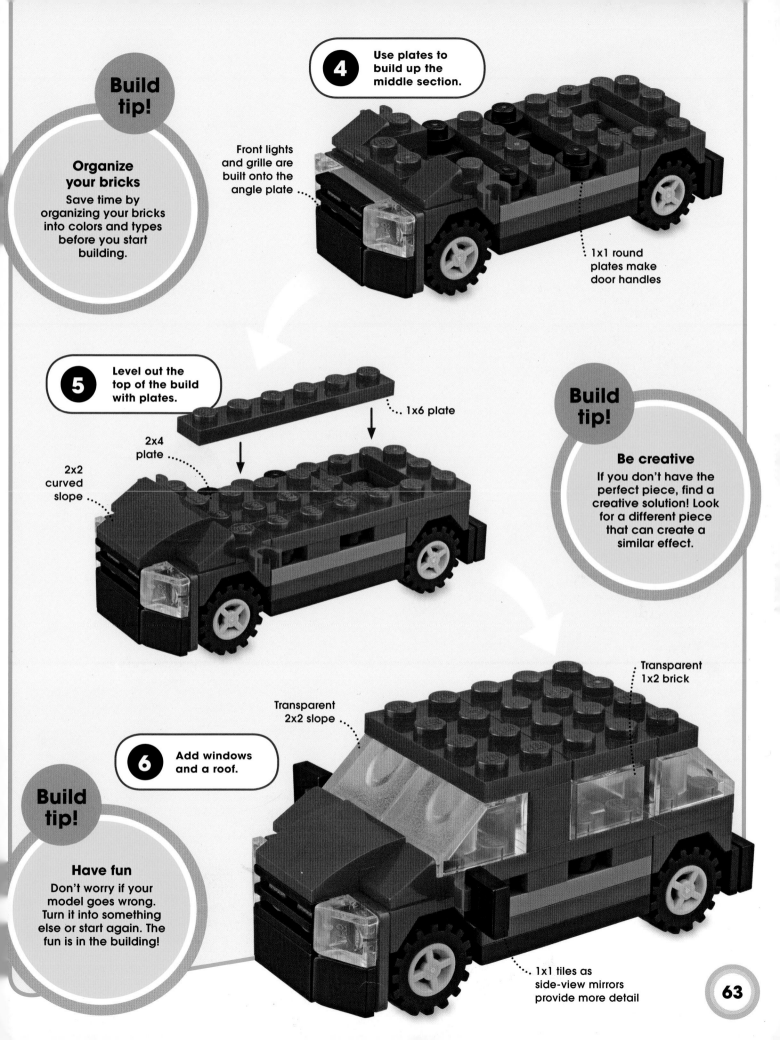

Meet the builders

The models in this book were created by a talented team of builders who are crazy about LEGO® bricks! We asked them to share some of their secrets . . .

Jumbo jet
(Barney Main)

Trading ship
(Simon Pickard)

Fishing trawler
(Jason Briscoe)

Barney Main

How many bricks do you own?
Just about the right amount! But never enough LEGO® Mixel™ eyes.

What is your favorite vehicle?
Hot air balloons are so majestic. They often fly right over our house.

What is the most challenging build you made for this book?
The catering truck has a scissor mechanism so the container can lift up to the plane. It was hard to make the container stay level and not wobble around.

What is your favorite build that you made for this book?
The jumbo jet. It's so sleek and swooshable! And I love the rich, dark blue trim.

What are your top tips for building vehicles?
Get the wheels right! You need big, chunky wheels for a monster truck and small, thin ones for a micro-scale

railroad carriage. Having the right wheels helps the rest of the model take shape. If it's got no wheels, pick another key feature— the propeller, or the wings, or the windshield, or the length of the boat. Then build from the bottom up on a nice big plate.

What is your favorite brick?
1x2 bow. It's really useful on small models for adding strength while keeping the model looking smooth.

If you could build any vehicle in the world, what would it be?
I'd love to build a helicopter from LEGO bricks that could actually fly!

Catering truck

64

Simon Pickard

How many bricks do you own?
More than two million!

What is your favorite vehicle?
17th-century sailing ships.

What is the most challenging build you made for this book?
The snowmobile. The smaller you get, the more difficult it becomes to build! I was very pleased with the look I still managed to get for this despite the challenging size.

What is your favorite build that you made for this book?
The 19th-century trading ship, because I love history, and the look of this ship at such a small scale really appeals to me.

What are your top tips for building vehicles?
Don't expect to get it right the first time. Sometimes you have to experiment a little to get the right look.

What is your favorite brick?
The 1x1 brick with studs all around, because it enables a wide range of complicated building techniques.

If you could build any vehicle in the world, what would it be?
A space rocket—because who doesn't want to go to space?

> Snowmobile

Jason Briscoe

> Road roller

What is the most challenging build you made for this book?
Probably the road roller, as I wanted to use the half cylinders and had to work up a design that looked right and made best use of the part.

What is your favorite build that you made for this book?
The fishing trawler. It has some really cool touches, like the red macaroni tubes on the roof.

What are your top tips for building vehicles?
Always revisit and rework your model. Often the best version will only come about by tinkering and modifying it until you can't do anymore to it.

What is your favorite brick?
That's a hard one! So many cool parts are released every year. My favorite right now is the 1x1 angled bracket, because it opens up new possibilities.

If you could build any vehicle in the world, what would it be?
A time machine. It would be great to visit the future and see what it holds!

How many bricks do you own?
Approximately two to three million—and counting!

Glossary

Propeller tilts up and down

Blimp

Pickup truck bed

Monster truck

Bumper guard

ROGER THAT!

Aluminum
A lightweight, silver-colored metal. Aluminum is commonly used to make vehicles.

Asteroid
A small, rocky object that orbits the Sun.

Bow
The forward end of a vessel, such as a ship.

Bridge
The area of a ship from which the captain or crew can navigate.

Capsize
To turn over in water.

Carbon fiber
A very strong, lightweight material that is often used to make vehicles, such as cars and airplanes.

Continuous track
A continuous band of track plates or treads that is driven by two or more wheels. The track helps vehicles, such as crawler cranes, grip all types of ground.

Conveyor belt
A continuous moving band of material, such as rubber, that transports objects from one place to another.

Diesel
A type of heavy oil that is used as fuel in some kinds of engines.

Ducted fan
A propeller housed inside a tube called a duct.

Efficient
To perform a function or job without wasting much effort and time.

Energy
The power that makes something, such as an engine, work.

Envelope
The fabric of a hot air balloon, which has an opening at the bottom and is attached to the basket of the balloon.

Equipment
A set of necessary objects or tools that are used for a specific purpose or job.

Fiberglass
A type of material made from plastic and glass fibers. Fiberglass is sometimes used to make vehicles.

Force
The pull or push on an object that causes it to move, slow down, or stay in place.

Fuselage
The main body of an aircraft, such as that of an airplane.

Gasoline
A type of lightweight oil that is used as fuel in some kinds of engines.

Passenger door

Fuselage

Early helicopter

Seaplane

Single propeller

Blade

Monoplane

Tail light

Red port light

Wheels for landing

Gravity
The force that pulls objects toward the center of the Earth. Gravity keeps objects from floating away.

Harbor
An area of water, often with piers or jetties, where boats can moor or dock.

Hull
The main body of a ship or other vessel. The hull is made up of the bottom, sides, and deck of a ship.

Hydraulic
A type of mechanical system that uses fluid to operate. Excavators and dump trucks use hydraulics to move parts of their machinery.

Maneuver
To move with skill and with care.

Monoplane
An airplane with only one set of wings.

Orbit
To travel around something. The Earth orbits the Sun.

Port
The left side of a vessel, such as a ship, when facing forward.

Pressure
The physical force put on an object by another object.

Rechargeable battery
A battery that can be charged with electricity more than once in order to give the battery energy again.

Solar system
The Sun and the eight planets, asteroids, comets, and other smaller bodies that orbit it.

Streamlined
An object that is designed to move very quickly through air or water.

Suspension
The system of tires, shock absorbers, and springs that connects a vehicle to its wheels. It helps to reduce the uncomfortable effects of bumps on the road.

Technology
Tools and devices that help people to do things, such as travel around, more easily.

Vehicle
An object that transports people, animals, or goods from one place to another.

Watertight
Sealed tightly so that no water can pass through.

MAYBE I SHOULD HAVE GONE BY TRAIN . . .

Hood

Corridor connector

High-speed train

Personal watercraft

Index

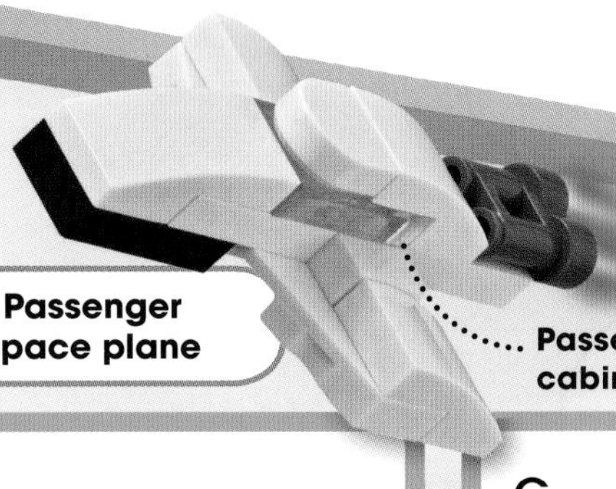

Rescue helicopter

Main rotor hub

Passenger space plane

Passenger cabin

Unmanned aerial vehicle

Battery

School bus

Door

Pilot

Unmanned aerial vehicle controller

Removable tail

Flying car

Safety helmet

I CAN'T DECIDE WHICH PAGE TO LAND ON!

Personal flyer

Mast

Fishing trawler

Anchor